S0-BSN-893

UNITED KINGDOM

by Bitsy Kemper

The Child's World

Published by The Child's World®
1980 Lookout Drive • Mankato, MN 56003-1705
800-599-READ • www.childsworld.com

Acknowledgments
The Child's World®: Mary Berendes, Publishing Director
Red Line Editorial: Editorial direction
The Design Lab: Design
Amnet: Production

Design elements: Bruce Stanfield/Shutterstock Images;
Asaf Eliason/Shutterstock Images; Andy Lidstone/
Shutterstock Images
Photographs ©: Bruce Stanfield/Shutterstock Images;
Asaf Eliason/Shutterstock Images; Andy Lidstone/
Shutterstock Images

ISBN 9781634070591
LCCN 2014959749

Printed in the United States of America
Mankato, MN
July, 2015
PA02268

ABOUT THE AUTHOR
Bitsy Kemper has written
more than a dozen books.
She's active in sports,
church, and theater
(but not all at the same
time). Kemper loves a
good laugh as much as
a good read. Busy with
three kids, she also
enjoys learning about new
cultures.

ONE WORLD • MANY COUNTRIES

TABLE OF CONTENTS

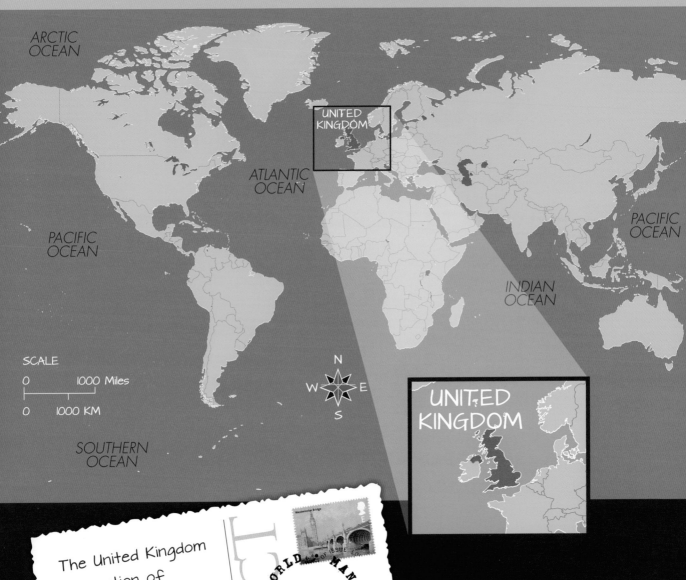

ARCTIC
OCEAN

UNITED
KINGDOM

ATLANTIC
OCEAN

PACIFIC
OCEAN

PACIFIC
OCEAN

INDIAN
OCEAN

SCALE

0   1000 Miles

0   1000 KM

N
W   E
S

SOUTHERN
OCEAN

UNITED
KINGDOM

The United Kingdom
is a nation of
islands. No place in
the United Kingdom
is more than 78
miles (125 km) from
the ocean.

FUN FACT

ONE WORLD • MANY COUNTRIES

CHAPTER 1

WELCOME TO THE UNITED KINGDOM!

The streets of West London are buzzing. The happy beat of a steel drum is pounding. Dancers in costumes ride on colorful floats. The smell of fresh Caribbean food fills the streets. About 1 million people are having a good time at the Notting Hill Carnival.

Girls participate in a parade during the Notting Hill Carnival.

This Carnival is the largest street festival in Europe. It celebrates Afro-Caribbean cultures and traditions. It is held over a long weekend every August. It reminds people of islands left behind.

People from Europe, Asia, and Africa live in London. More than 3 million Londoners are from different parts of the world. The mix of people creates a lively city.

London is the capital of both England and the United Kingdom. The United Kingdom's official name is the United Kingdom of Great Britain and Northern Ireland. For short, most people call it the United Kingdom or the UK. The United Kingdom

contains three separate countries and one **province**. The countries are England, Scotland, and Wales. Northern Ireland is the province. Citizens are called British, or Brits.

In the 1800s, the British Empire stretched over a quarter of Earth's surface. Today's United Kingdom is a little smaller than the state of Michigan. More than 64 million people call it home.

London is always busy. It is famous for its red, double-decker buses.

CHAPTER 2

THE LAND

The English countryside has gentle, rolling hills and lakes. The high rainfall each year makes the land green.

The United Kingdom is made up of islands. The largest island is Great Britain. It is home to England, Scotland, and Wales. Northern Ireland is part of the island to the west of Great Britain. Northern Ireland, England, Scotland, and Wales all form the United Kingdom.

Northern Ireland is not the same as Ireland. It is a small part of Ireland. The province is about the size of Maryland. The rest of the island is the Republic of Ireland. It is a different country under its own rule.

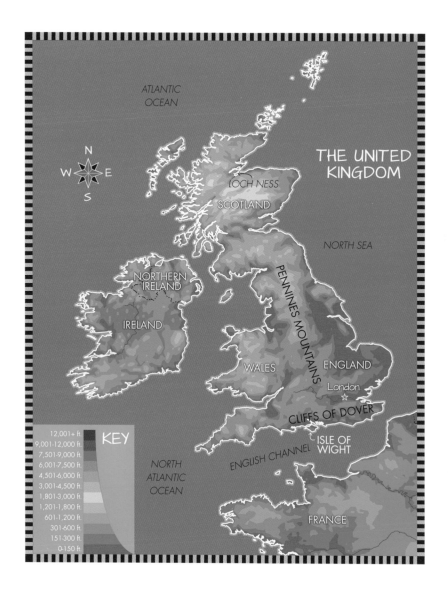

The United Kingdom is part of Europe. France and Ireland
are its nearest neighbors. The United Kingdom is between the
North Atlantic Ocean and the North Sea. The water between
Great Britain and France is called the English Channel. The
United Kingdom is connected to Europe's mainland by an
underground train tunnel.

Dover is famous for its white cliffs. They are made of chalk, which gives them their white color.

England covers most of Great Britain. It has about 1,000 smaller islands off its coast. The largest is the Isle of Wight.

The Pennines Mountains run through the north of England. They span almost 250 miles (400 km). Tall cliffs are in the southeast. The most famous are the Cliffs of Dover.

The weather in England is mild. It does not get too hot or too cold. It snows every year, but only a little. It rains throughout the year. The wet weather keeps the land green. But that means the sun is not shining for more than half of the year.

Scotland's land varies. The north is rocky, and the south is flat. There are several lakes, called lochs. The most famous is Loch Ness. Scotland also has 790 islands, most of which are **uninhabited**. Winters in Scotland are a bit colder than the rest of the United Kingdom. The north gets more snow than the south. Both areas get rain all year.

Wales has mountains and farmlands. The weather gets cool in winter and warm in summer. It rains a little more than in England.

Scotland's Loch Ness is a long, narrow lake. According to legend, the Loch Ness Monster lives there.

Northern Ireland is hilly. It has mountains and rivers. It also has a flat fruit-growing region. Overall it gets less sun and more rain than the other countries.

The green lands of the United Kingdom have many resources. They have coal, petroleum, and natural gas. These **fossil fuels** are important around the world. They are used to produce heat and electricity.

The "British Isles" is a name used for the United Kingdom. It describes all the islands in the area. It includes the islands of Great Britain, Ireland, and close to 5,000 smaller islands.

FUN FACT

ONE WORLD · MANY COUNTRIES

CHAPTER 3

GOVERNMENT AND CITIES

London, England, is the capital of the United Kingdom. More than 9 million people live there. It has many landmarks. The queen lives in London's Buckingham Palace. A large clock called Big Ben rises over the city. The Tower Bridge spans the River Thames. The London Eye is one of the world's tallest Ferris wheels.

The River Thames flows through London. The Tower Bridge can move higher and lower to allow large ships to pass under it.

Edinburgh's skyline has a mix of modern and historic buildings.

Each country in the United Kingdom has a capital. Edinburgh is Scotland's capital. It is on the shores of the Firth of Forth, which is part of the North Sea.

Cardiff is the capital and largest city in Wales. The city has existed since the year 75 AD, but it did not become the capital until 1955. It is the youngest capital city in Europe.

Belfast is the capital and biggest city of Northern Ireland. Close to 280,000 people live there. The RMS *Titanic* passenger ship was built there. The famous author C.S. Lewis was from Belfast.

The United Kingdom's countries are broken into smaller areas, similiar to states. England, Northern Ireland, and Wales have counties and **boroughs**. Scotland's states are called council areas. Each area plays a part in government.

1. Greater Manchester
2. West Yorkshire
3. South Yorkshire
4. Nottinghamshire
5. Staffordshire
6. Warwickshire
7. Northamptonshire
8. Cambridgeshire
9. Buckingham
10. Buckinghamshire
11. Glouchestershire
12. West Glamorgan
13. Mid Glamorgan
14. South Glamorgan
15. Magherafelt
16. Castlereagh
17. Craigavon

THE UNITED KINGDOM

NORTH ATLANTIC OCEAN

NORTH SEA

NORTHERN IRELAND

BELFAST

IRELAND

Western Isles Area

Orkney Islands Area

Highland   Grampian

Tayside

Central   Fife

GLASGOW   EDINBURGH

Lothian

Strathclyde   Borders

Dumfries and Galloway   Northumberland

Tyne and Wear

Durham   Cleveland

Cumbria

North Yorkshire

Lancashire   Humberside

Merseyside

Cheshire   Derby   2   Lincolnshire

Clwyd   1   3

Gwynedd   5   4

Shropshire   Leicestershire   Norfolk

Powys   7   8

Worcester   6   Suffolk

Dyfed   10   9   Essex

Gwent   11   Oxford   LONDON

12   13

14   Berkshire

CARDIFF   Bristol   Surrey   Kent

Wiltshire

Somerset   Hampshire   West Sussex   East Sussex

Devon   Dorset

Isle of Wight

Cornwall

ENGLISH CHANNEL

FRANCE

NORTHERN IRELAND

Coleraine   Moyle

Limavady   Ballymoney   Larne

Londonderry   Ballymena   North Down

Strabane   15   Antrim

Omagh   Cookstown   16

Dungannon   Lisburn   Ards

17

Fermanagh   Banbridge   Down

Armagh   Newry and Mourne

15

The government is a commonwealth **monarchy**. That means they have a queen or a king. Elizabeth II has been Queen of the United Kingdom since 1952. In 2014, she started sharing duties with her son, Charles. He is next in line to become king.

Charles' oldest son is William. Prince William is the Duke of Cambridge. His wife, Kate, is the Duchess of Cambridge. William and Kate have traveled the world as future leaders.

Kings and queens are born into royal rule, not elected.

Queen Elizabeth II represents the United Kingdom when she travels to other parts of the world.

They act as heads of state. They do not make laws or run the government. Making laws is the work of **parliament**. The UK's parliament is run by a prime minister. Citizens of the United Kingdom elect the prime minister.

The United Kingdom's **economy** is strong. It sells fossil fuels to other countries. Factories in the United Kingdom build cars, such as Land Rovers and Mini Coopers. The United Kingdom also produces software, ships, aircraft, and clothing.

Lawmakers meet in London at the House of Parliament. It is on the River Thames.

The United Kingdom's currency

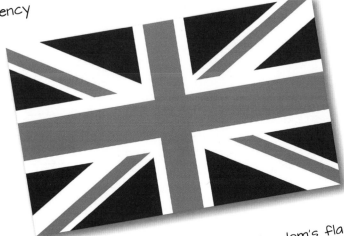

The United Kingdom's flag

Money in the United Kingdom is called the pound. The sign for the pound is £. To avoid confusion between the money and the weight, the money is called the "pound sterling" or simply "sterling." In slang it is called "quid."

FUN FACT

ONE WORLD • MANY COUNTRIES

GLOBAL CONNECTIONS

The United Kingdom, and England especially, had a major influence on all parts of the globe. In the 1600s, British sailors began to claim islands and other countries for England. The lands they claimed became part of the British Empire.

From the 1700s until the mid-1900s, the British Empire was the largest empire in the world. It included parts of Africa, India, Australia, and the Americas.

The English influenced the countries in the empire. In many colonies, people adopted the English language. People often began dressing like the English, rather than wearing traditional clothing. English leaders set up modern schools and clinics like those in England.

"The sun never sets on the British Empire" used to be a popular saying. That is because it was always daylight somewhere in their empire. Today, the United Kingdom still has 14 overseas territories. They include Canada, Jamaica, and Australia. These countries are independent, but they still have a close connection to the United Kingdom.

CHAPTER 4

PEOPLE AND CULTURES

People have settled in the United Kingdom for thousands of years. Anglo-Saxons, Celts, and Jutes were early groups to settle there. Later, Normans from France, Romans from Italy, and Vikings from Norway arrived. Today, the United Kingdom has citizens from all over the world.

Some children from the United Kingdom can trace their roots back thousands of years.

People in the United Kingdom speak English. Some English words are different between the United States and the United Kingdom. Brits call the television the "telly." An elevator is a "lift." The trunk of a car is the "boot."

People of the United Kingdom speak other languages, too. About 30 percent of people in Scotland speak Scottish. In Wales, about 20 percent of people speak Welsh. Close to 10 percent of people in Northern Ireland speak Irish. And in south England, about 2,000 people speak Cornish.

At the London Underground train, signs warn riders to "mind the gap." This phrase means "watch your step."

The United Kingdom has many daily customs, such as afternoon tea. Traditionally, tea was served as an afternoon snack. Proper table manners were required. The food included sandwiches, small cakes, and tea. Many Brits today still enjoy an afternoon tea, but it is no longer so formal.

Holidays are important in the United Kingdom. Instead of "going on vacation," Brits "take a holiday." What the United States calls a holiday, the United Kingdom calls a "bank holiday." Both mean a day off from school or work. Bank holidays include

New Year's Day, Good Friday, Easter Monday, Christmas, and Boxing Day.

January 25 in Scotland is Burns Night. It celebrates the Scottish poet Robert Burns. Men wear **kilts**. People play bagpipes. Sheep hearts, liver, and lungs are chopped up for a traditional dish called *haggis*.

March 1 is Saint David's Day in Wales. The saint brought Christianity to the country and built churches. Parades, concerts, and parties are held in his honor.

Saint Patrick's Day is on March 17. It is a bank

Afternoon tea is a way to take a break and slow down during a busy day.

holiday only in Northern Ireland. But the whole United Kingdom celebrates. The day honors Saint Patrick. He brought Christianity to Ireland in the 400s. At first, Saint Patrick's Day was a religious holiday in the Republic of Ireland. Today, it is a celebration of Irish culture around the world.

The United Kingdom is famous for its writers, including William Shakespeare. Many people consider Shakespeare the greatest English writer in history. Shakespeare lived from 1554 to 1616. During his life he wrote 37 plays and more than 150 poems.

FUN FACT

ONE WORLD · MANY COUNTRIES

Westminster Bridge

CHAPTER 5

DAILY LIFE

In many ways, daily life in the United Kingdom is similar to that in other parts of Europe. Homes, clothing, and cars are modern. Most children attend school, and parents often work.

A traditional meal is fish and chips, which is fried fish and French fries. Indian food is popular, too. Afternoon tea is held informally in most homes, with hot tea and small snacks.

Eating fish and chips by the sea

Other than school uniforms, British children dress like most children in the United States. Blue jeans, T-shirts, and sneakers are popular. Sneakers, called trainers, are sized differently from the United States. A boy's size 13 shoe would be a size 30 in the United Kingdom.

Cars and driving in the United Kingdom are different than in many other parts of the world. In the United Kingdom a car's steering wheel is on the right side of the car. Cars drive on the left side of the road.

Many Londoners rely on public transportation. The main train system is called the Underground, or the Tube.

A train, taxi, bus, tram, or river taxi are the fastest ways to get around. Most people outside of cities drive personal vehicles. About 75 percent of homes have at least one car.

Another important part of daily life are social gatherings. Early spring through summer is known as "the season." Nearly 1.3 million people from all over go to social events. People attend concerts, teas, polo matches, and yacht races at this time.

The United Kingdom is a country with a long

Steering wheels in cars in the United Kingdom are on the right side of the car.

Many people from the United Kingdom are proud of their country.

history. Its empire once stretched across much of the globe and influenced many countries. Today, the United Kingdom no longer controls an empire, but it is still an important world leader.

DAILY LIFE FOR CHILDREN

In the United Kingdom, students go to school and learn history, science, and other subjects. Gym class might include a game called cricket. Cricket uses equipment called wickets, stumps, and bails. It is similar to baseball. Gym classes might play soccer, which the British call football. Both sports are popular.

After school, kids might watch telly or play computer games. Dinner is around 6:30 p.m. It might be fish sticks, called fish fingers, served with peas. England has a large population of people with Indian heritage. Many Indian foods are part of the British diet. Dinner might be chicken tikka masala, an Indian dish made with a creamy and spicy sauce.

A tunnel connects England and France. It is called the Channel Tunnel. The tunnel runs under the English Channel for 31 miles (50 km). Riders can board a train in Folkestone, England, to travel to Coquelles, France.

FUN FACT

ONE WORLD · MANY COUNTRIES

FAST FACTS

Population: 63 million

Area: 94,100 square miles (243,610 sq km)

Capital: London, England

Largest Cities: London, England; Glasgow, Scotland; Cardiff, Wales; and Belfast, Northern Ireland

Form of Government: Constitutional Monarchy

Languages: English, with some regional languages

Trading Partners: Germany, the United States, China, and the Netherlands

Major Holidays: Christmas, New Year's Day, Notting Hill Carnival, Burn's Night, Saint David's Day, and Saint Patrick's Day

National Dishes: Fish and chips, and chicken tikka masala

Big Ben is the nickname of the large clock in London. In 2012, it was officially named the Elizabeth Tower.

GLOSSARY

boroughs (BUHR-ohs) Boroughs are towns or villages that have their own governments. England, Northern Ireland, and Wales are made up of boroughs.

economy (ih-KON-uh-me) An economy is how a country runs its industry, trade, and finance. The United Kingdom has a strong economy.

fossil fuels (FOSS-il FYOO-uhlz) Fossil fuels are coal, oil, or natural gas, which formed over time from the remains of ancient plants and animals. Many fossil fuels are used to make electricity and heat.

kilts (KILTZ) Kilts are traditional pleated plaid skirts worn by Scottish men. Kilts are worn for special occasions. Scottish men wear kilts on holidays.

monarchy (MON-ur-kee) A monarchy is a form of government based upon a king or queen. The head of the British monarchy is Queen Elizabeth II.

parliament (PAR-luh-muhnt) A parliament is a group of elected officials who make the laws in certain countries. The UK parliament is run by the prime minister.

province (PROV-uhnss) A province is a district or region of some countries. Northern Ireland is a province of the United Kingdom.

uninhabited (un-en-HA-buh-tud) Uninhabited means having no people or animals living there. Some of the islands in the United Kingdom are uninhabited.

To Learn More

BOOKS

Dillon, Patrick. *The Story of Britain*. Somerville: Candlewick Press, 2011.

Scott, Janine. *Not-for-Parents Great Britain: Everything You Wanted to Know*. Footscray, Australia: Lonely Planet, 2012.

The United Kingdom: England. New York: Britannica Educational Publishing, 2014.

WEB SITES

Visit our Web site for links about the United Kingdom:
childsworld.com/links

Note to Parents, Teachers, and Librarians: We routinely verify our Web links to make sure they are safe and active sites. So encourage your readers to check them out!

Index